The Guardian Angel's Adventure

Written by
Rev. Jose Kallukalam

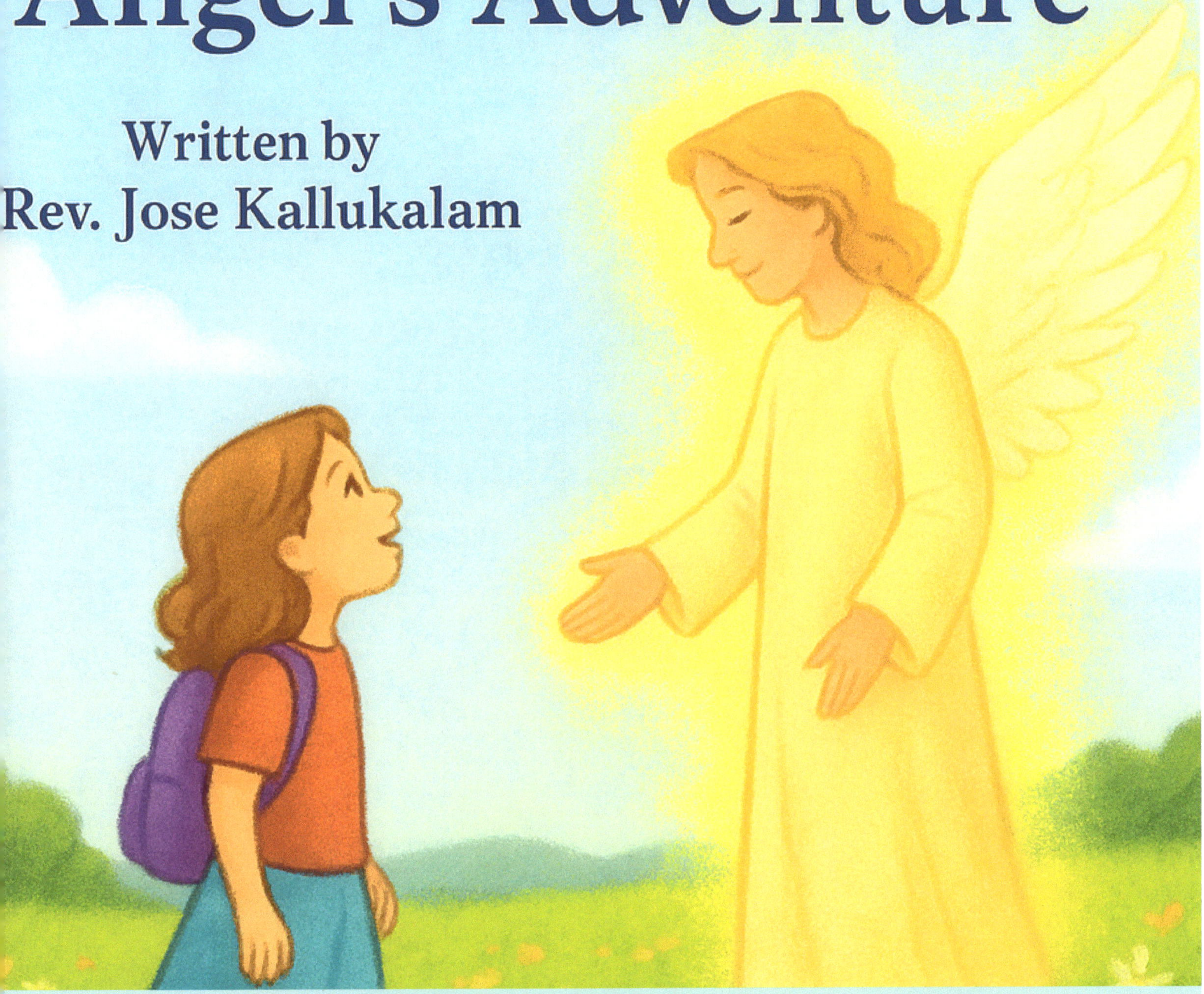

Children's Story Picture Book

The Guardian Angel's Adventure

Rev. Jose Kallukalam

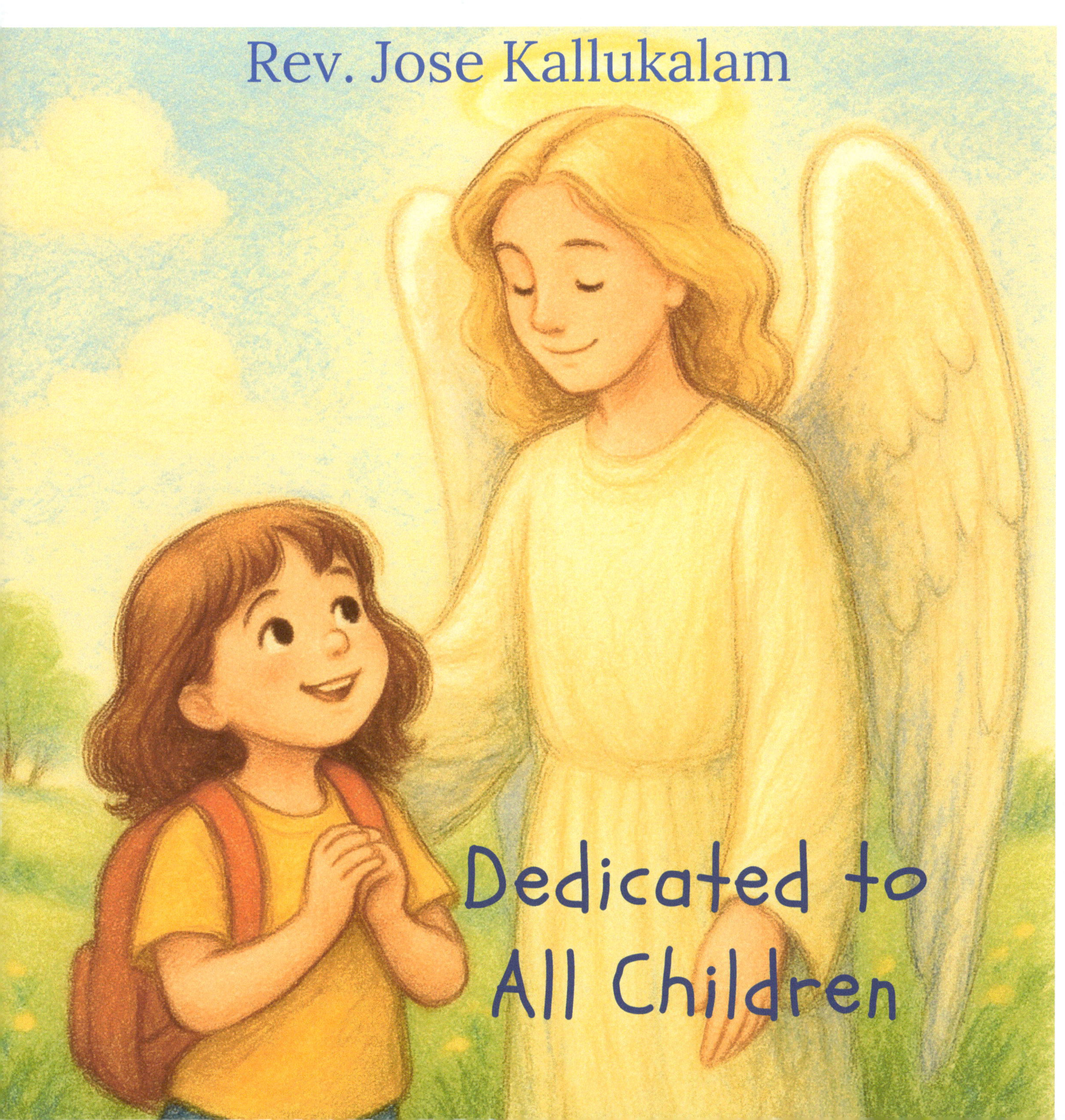

Chapter 1
Wake Up, Little Hero

"Psst... time to wake up, sleepyhead!"

the guardian angel whispered.

"It's your big day—

your very first day of school."

The little girl groaned

and pulled the blanket over her head.

The guardian angel grinned.

"Even heroes need to brush their teeth

before saving the world."

Wait. A hero's first mission is to say good morning to God.

"Good morning, God. Please be with me today.

She hopped out of bed

and hurried toward the bathroom.

"Wait," said the guardian angel gently.

"A hero's first mission is

to say good morning to God."

She stopped,

folded her hands,

and whispered:

"Good morning, God.

Please be with me today."

The guardian angel's wings

sparkled with joy.

Chapter 3
Breakfast Chaos

Downstairs,

her toast popped up

black as a shoe!

"Yuck," she said, frowning.

The guardian angel chuckled.

"Oops, even toast can have a bad day.

Heroes eat around the edges."

She giggled, took a bite,

and prayed,

"Thank You, God, for breakfast—

even the crunchy parts."

Chapter 4
Walking to School

The little girl

tugged at her heavy backpack.

Her shoes scraped the sidewalk.

She whispered,

"What if I don't make any friends?"

The guardian angel

walked beside her and smiled.

"Don't be afraid.

I'll walk with you every step."

Her shoulders lifted,

and she took a braver step forward.

Chapter 5
At the School Gate

At the tall school gate,

children laughed and shouted.

The girl's knees felt wobbly.

The guardian angel whispered,

"Take a deep breath.
Heroes are strong inside."

The girl squeezed

the straps of her backpack.

She whispered,

"Okay... I can do this."

And she walked through the gate.

Chapter 6
First Classroom Moment

The classroom was noisy
with new voices.

The teacher smiled and said,

"Class, this is Anna."

Anna's cheeks grew red as apples.

The guardian angel leaned close

and whispered,

"Don't worry. God made you special.

Every friend you haven't met yet

is waiting to smile back."

Anna lifted her hand in a shy wave.

A boy at the front desk waved back.

Chapter 7
Playground Trouble

At recess,

kids ran across the playground

playing tag.

Anna stood by the slide, hugging her arms.

"They won't let me in," she whispered.

The guardian angel chuckled kindly.

"Heroes don't give up after one try.

Ask again—and remember,

God made you brave."

Anna took a deep breath.

"Can I play?" she asked.

"Sure!" shouted the children,

and they pulled her into the game.

Chapter 8
Lunchtime Mix-Up

Anna's sandwich slipped from her hands

and landed in the dirt.

Her face turned red.

She wanted to cry.

The girl sitting next to her

smiled kindly.

"Here—take half of mine," she said,

breaking her sandwich in two.

Anna's eyes lit up.

The guardian angel beamed.

"See, that is real love—sharing."

Anna smiled.

"What do you tell your friend?" Angel asked.

Anna said, "Thank you."

Both girls laughed and munched together.

Chapter 9
A Hurt Feeling

Later,

a boy said something unkind.

Anna's fists tightened.

She wanted to snap back.

The guardian angel

whispered softly,

"Words can sting—or heal.

Which one will you choose?

What would Jesus do?"

Anna took a deep breath.

She offered a small smile instead

and whispered, "Forgive."

Chapter 10
Afternoon Challenge

The teacher pointed to the board.

"Who can solve this problem?" she asked.

Anna's heart thumped.

Her hand felt heavy.

The guardian angel leaned close

and whispered,

"Even if it's wrong,

it's brave to try.

God loves courage."

Anna raised her hand slowly.

Her answer was right!

The class clapped.

Anna's smile stretched

as wide as the chalkboard.

Chapter 11
End of the Day

The bell rang.

Backpacks zipped.

Chairs squeaked.

Anna rubbed her tired eyes but grinned.

The teacher said,

"Anna, you were kind and brave today."

The guardian angel leaned close and asked,

"What do you say to the teacher?"

Anna's smile grew wide.
"Thank you, Teacher."

The guardian angel clapped
his glowing hands.

"See? You made it through.

God is proud of you."

Anna skipped toward the door,

lighter than her backpack.

Chapter 12
Walking Home

Anna skipped along the sidewalk,

her backpack bouncing.

"How was school, Anna?"
Her mom asked.

"Today wasn't so scary after all,"
she said.

Her mom smiled,

listening as Anna told her stories.

The guardian angel walked beside them,

glowing like sunset.

"See?" the angel whispered.

"Heroes wear backpacks too."

Anna giggled.

Chapter 13
Evening Prayer

At bedtime,

Anna folded her hands.

"Thank You, God,

for my Mom and Dad,

for my teacher, my friends,

and my sandwich," she whispered.

The guardian angel knelt beside her.

"Every prayer is a gift.

God loves hearing your voice."

Anna smiled and whispered softly

"Good night, Jesus."

Her eyes grew heavy with peace.

Chapter 14
Closing Blessing

The guardian angel leaned close

and whispered,

"I'll watch over you all night.

Tomorrow brings
another adventure."

Anna drifted to sleep,

hugging her pillow.

She then whispered,

"Thank you God
for my Guardian Angel."

Her angel smiled

and spread the glowing wings
like a blanket of light.

A Prayer to the Guardian Angel

"Angel of God,

my guardian dear,

to whom God's love

entrusts me here,

ever this day be at my side,

to light and guard,

to protect and guide.

Amen."